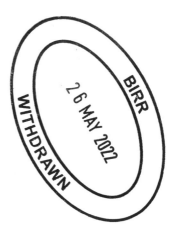
SLICED IN TWO

D0308726

WAYLAND
www.waylandbooks.co.uk

First published in 2013 by Wayland

Wayland
338 Euston Road
London NW1 3BH

Wayland Australia
Level 17/207 Kent Street
Sydney, NSW 2000

Series Editor: Louise John
Series design: Robert Walster
Design: Lisa Peacock
Consultant: Fiona Collins

A CIP catalogue record for this book is available
from the British Library.

ISBN 9780750268967

Printed in China

Wayland is a division of Hachette Children's Books,
an Hachette UK Company

www.hachette.co.uk

Sliced in Two

Andrew Fusek Peters
and Cathy Brett

Titles in the series

The Crawling Hand

9780750268950

Sliced in Two

9780750268967

Wolf Boy

9780750268974

High Stakes

9780750268981

CHAPTER 1

The huge saws screamed as they cut the wooden beam. But something else was screaming. Polly pushed up her safety goggles to look. A man walked towards her. He had been cut in half, from his head right down to his feet. Blood dripped from his legs as they came closer and closer. His staring eyes shone with tears. His mouth was open in a scream. Polly joined in with a scream of her own. Then she fainted.

A while later, my uncle Ali, who was the manager of the woodyard, handed Polly a cup of tea.

"I don't see why we're here, Ali?" said Polly. It was a good question. She huddled in the corner, sipping her

7

tea with shaking hands. Uncle Ali frowned. "The woodyard should be a safe place to work. Now this happens! I told the police, but they weren't interested!" he said.

Sam leaned forward in her chair.

"Not surprising! They don't believe in ghosts."

"Neither do I," I said.

"I know what I saw," Polly muttered to herself.

"Yes. It's the last thing I need. The wood yard is going to be bought and we'll all lose our jobs. Now, it seems I'm going crazy as well. I've heard you're good at this sort of

problem, Jas?" asked Ali.

"Sure!" I said. "Our last case involved a bunch of skeletons. Ghosts are easy."

Later that night, the place was ours. The saws were silent.

"What do you think?" asked Sam.

Well, I thought that Sam was looking pretty gorgeous. But I didn't say anything.

At that moment there was a whisper in the shadows. A stain spread across the concrete floor. Under the lamplight it looked red. And sticky.

13

"I think we've got company!"
Sam hissed at me.

The hairs on the back of my neck
stood up and my heart began to race.

CHAPTER 2

"OMG!" I whimpered. It was just like Polly had said.

"Totally sliced in half!" Sam said to herself.

"He tied me up and got out his saw!" the ghost wailed.

I tried not to be sick. "Who did?"

"Tom Jones!" said the ghost.

"The singer?" asked Sam.

"No. But that was his name!
Everyone teased him. They'd say,

'Give us a song, Tom!'"

By now the ghost was quite close. The smell was rank – rotten wood and death. It was odd seeing his insides. "You don't look well," I said.

"Don't feel it either," the ghost said. "I'm Jack, by the way."

Sam was already on the case. "So, why did Tom kill you, Jack?"

"Caught him working extra jobs at night. He was making a fortune.

I was the only one who knew.
So he sliced me in two," said the
ghost sadly.

"And now, you're not half the man
you were!" said Sam.

Jack stared at her.

"Sorry," said Sam. "Bad joke."

I felt sorry for the guy. "How long ago was this?"

"Twenty years. And he's been growing richer every day. Now he's

bought the woodyard and is going
to get rid of my body so no one will
find out what he did. I won't let him."
Each half of Jack began to shake
and sob.

"Get a hold of yourself," said Sam. "We're here to help."

Suddenly, the ghost vanished and a pair of meaty hands grabbed hold of me.

"What the…?" I cried.

"Shut it!" a voice said.

Before I knew what was going on, the world went dark.

CHAPTER 3

"Urrrr!" I mumbled. I was still so sleepy. Then a bright light came on and I opened my eyes.

The first thing I saw was Sam tied to a chair.

"If you've hurt her, I'm going to kill

you!" I shouted.

"How very loyal of you," a posh voice answered. An old man was standing next to a large gas bottle. "Let me introduce myself," he said.

"Give us a song, Tom," I said as I tried to wriggle free of my ropes.

The man scowled. "Seems that you have a brain. Pity you won't have

time to use it." He played with the top
of the gas bottle.

I couldn't help myself. "Why?"

"Meddling with me is not a good
idea. This bottle contains toxic gas.
Once the wood yard is mine, an old

matter shall be taken care of once
and for all. Happy breathing." He
walked towards the door.

"You're going to kill a couple of
kids?" I gasped.

"Don't take it the wrong way. It's
just business. Goodbye!"

The gas bottle hissed. I began to feel sleepy again. I looked at Sam.

"I swear, if I ever get us out of this, I'm going to kiss you," I said to her quietly.

Stupid promise, really. We were about to die.

CHAPTER 4

"Young man!" It was a whisper in my ear.

"What? Let me sleep!"

"No. You must wake up."

I pulled my eyelids open. The two halves of Jack were looking at the

chair that I was tied to.

"It's made from wood," he said. "There's a weak spot by your elbow. Give it a shove, eh?"

I did as I was told. There was a crack as the chair broke.

I pulled off the ropes and ran over to
Sam. "Wake up, girl!"

Sam moaned, then slowly opened
her eyes.

"Where am I?"

I began to undo the knots. "Miles
from the action. We need to hit the

wood yard, quick."

As we ran down the corridor, I shouted to Jack. "Why couldn't you stop him turning on the gas bottle?"

"I'm a ghost, remember?" said Jack. "Trying to turn off the gas bottle

would be like trying to butter the air."

"And," said Sam, "he's a bit half-hearted!"

Nobody laughed. We sprinted round the corner. Right into the arms of the thug who had grabbed me earlier.

"Going somewhere?" he snarled.

"They're with me!" wailed Jack.
His two halves began to bleed and
maggots crawled round the edges of
the cut.

One look at Jack, and the two men screamed and ran.

"Nice one, mate!" said Sam.

"It's a scary business. But someone's gotta do it!" Jack smiled.

As we left the building to head across town, Sam took out her mobile and lifted it to her ear.

"What are you doing?" I asked.

"Back-up!" said Sam. "Trust me."

CHAPTER 5

Back at the wood yard, Jack took
us into the corner of an old shed.

"That's where I am. He stuck my
body in the ground, just under
the floorboards."

Sam looked at me. "We're going to

need a crowbar."

"Why do you always boss me around?"

"Because it's fun. And I like it." Sam grinned at me. Boy, she could be a pain.

"Ooof," I found a crowbar and got
the first floorboard up.

A torch shone into my face.
I was blinded.

"Well, well. Look who we
have here."

I knew that voice. "Tom Jones."

"The one and only. Carry on digging. It will save me getting my hands dirty. Once the body is uncovered, I can get rid of it."

"And what if I attack you?" I said, my voice shaking.

"Oh, how sweet. A fourteen-year-old threatening me. However, I do have this!" The light came on. Tom Jones had a gun in his hand.

"You do know you're surrounded?" said Sam calmly.

"This is not a book!" he snarled. "Do you think the police will rescue you?"

"Yes. Seeing as I asked nicely. And because they're armed."

Just at that moment, a voice blared out. "Put down your gun!"

Tom Jones grabbed my neck. I felt metal on my cheek. "Try anything and he gets it!"

I tried not to wet myself.

The police backed off. One of them dropped his gun.

For a second, Tom looked away. It was enough. Sam sprang into action. One kick and the gun flew out of Tom's hand. A punch to the stomach and he doubled over, letting go of me.

It was done. As Tom Jones lay on the floor, he was handcuffed. Sam smiled at me. "That thing you said."

"What thing?"

"That if we got through this, you'd give me a kiss."

"Oh. Yes. Erm."

Somewhere nearby a siren went off. A police officer grabbed Sam to shake her by the hand. I was safe, for now.

As for poor old Jack? They dug him

up and gave him a proper funeral.
Nothing half-hearted about it. Uncle
Ali was happy.

The cash reward was handy, but
the important thing was that the job
was done. And me and Sam? Did we
kiss? Now, that would be telling.

FOR TEACHERS

About

Freestylers is a series of carefully levelled stories, especially geared for struggling readers of both sexes. With very low reading age and high interest age, these books are humorous, fun, up-to-the-minute and edgy. Core characters provide familiarity in all of the stories, build confidence and ease pupils from one story through to the next, accelerating reading progress.

Freestylers can be used for both guided and independent reading. To make the most of the books you can:

• Focus on making each reading session successful. Talk about the text before the pupil starts reading. Introduce the characters, the storyline and any unfamiliar vocabulary.

• Encourage the pupil to talk about the book during reading and after reading. How would they have felt if they were Jas? Or Sam? How would they have gone about solving the mystery?

• Talk about which parts of the story they like best and why.

For guidance, this story has been approximately measured to:

National Curriculum Level: 2A
Reading Age: 7
Book Band: Lime

ATOS: 2.5
Lexile ® Measure [confirmed]: 340L